This book belongs to

_____

_____

Aged _____

# THE
# *House That Grew*

## AND OTHER STORIES

# THE
# *House That Grew*

## AND OTHER STORIES

*p*

This is a Parragon Book
This edition published in 2001

Parragon
Queen Street House
4 Queen Street
Bath BA1 1HE, UK

Copyright © Parragon 2000

ISBN 0-75253-413-0

Designed by Mik Martin

Printed in Italy

These stories have been previously
published by Parragon in the
Bumper Bedtime Series 1999

# CONTENTS

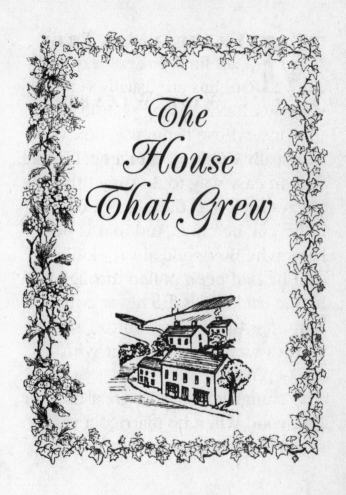

# The House That Grew

MANY YEARS AGO, there lived a goblin who was lazy. Goblins are usually very vigorous, hardworking people, but this one, whose name was Boxwood, was really not very energetic. If there was an easy way to do something, he always took it. If there was a corner to be cut, he cut it. And that is perhaps why Boxwood always looked as if he had been pulled through a hedge backwards. He never could be bothered to sew on a button, so his clothes were held together with safety pins.

Things improved a great deal for Boxwood when he married a very sensible goblin called Dahlia. She soon smartened Boxwood up and made his home, which had not really been the kind of place you would want to visit, into a little palace.

Pretty soon, Dahlia's and Boxwood's first baby arrived. It was a little boy, and you have never seen a prouder father than Boxwood. A couple of years later, a little girl was born. Boxwood was beside himself with joy. But when Dahlia had twins the following year, Boxwood's delight was tinged with anxiety. It was all right now, when the children were still quite tiny, but where would they sleep when they were older?

Now, a sensible goblin would

have done as Dahlia suggested and built an extension on to the back of the house. But Boxwood still had moments when he was not a very sensible goblin. He felt sure that there must be an easier way to make home improvements.

A few days later, Boxwood had the glimmering of an idea. He hurried down to the Lending Library to see if he could find some more

information. But he was disappointed. There were lots of books on do-it-yourself but none mentioned what Boxwood had in mind. He knew that he would have to go to an expert.

Old Millet lived by the stream that wound through the goblin town. He was a wise old goblin, with a friendly face. He was said to be wiser and cleverer than any goblin before him. And what was more, he was one of the few goblins who still remembered how to do magic.

There was a time when goblins used magic a great deal, but magic is dangerous stuff in the wrong hands. After some quite awful disasters, it was decided by the Goblin Council that only one goblin in each town or village would be allowed to practise magic, and that would be the wisest, most sensible goblin found to be living there.

Gradually, however, the use of magic almost died out. That was because wise, sensible goblins draw the line at using magic to do homework, brew up a love potion, or paint another goblin's house purple for a joke.

Somehow, the fun had gone out of magic, and it was very little used.

Boxwood arrived at Millet's house early one morning. He was polite and well dressed, so Millet, who didn't get out much any more, didn't realise quite what a silly goblin Boxwood was.

When Millet's visitor explained that he wanted to extend his house because of his growing family, the old goblin thought that sounded an excellent idea.

"But why can't you employ a builder?" he asked, reasonably.

"It's all the dust and dirt and

upheaval," sighed Boxwood. "My dear wife has four little children to look after. I don't think she could cope with building work on top of everything else."

Of course, the real reason was that Boxwood couldn't be bothered to do things properly, but Millet had

recently had his bathroom improved, so he knew exactly what Boxwood was talking about. He could well imagine that anyone would want to avoid unnecessary mess and fuss.

"So you'd like a spell to extend your house?" he asked.

"Yes, please," said Boxwood. "Just one extra room for the children should be enough."

"No problem," said Millet.

He went away into his study. Boxwood could hear muttering and the scratching of a pen. Minutes passed — many, many minutes. Boxwood, who was not a patient goblin at the best of times, began gnawing his knuckles in frustration.

Just when Boxwood thought he would give up the whole idea, Millet reappeared, clutching a piece of parchment.

"Thanks very much," cried Boxwood, seizing it. "Sorry I can't stay longer, but I've got to fly!"

"But…" cried Millet, "I haven't told you how to use the spell. That's most important. You could have a terrible accident."

Silly Boxwood was already halfway down the path. He didn't think he needed any further instructions. It was just a question of saying the spell, wasn't it?

Well, saying a spell is a little like using a recipe in cooking. It may be all right if you just follow the instructions, but quite a lot of common sense is needed as well. And as we know, Boxwood didn't have very much of that!

When Boxwood got home, Dahlia had gone to visit her mother with the children. With the house to himself, there was nothing to stop Boxwood trying out the spell. He looked at it carefully, but it seemed very straightforward. What could possibly go wrong?

Concentrating hard, for he knew it was important to get the words right, Boxwood read out the spell. He turned around twice after the third line and turned back again after the seventh line. Of course, if Boxwood had waited to hear what Millet had to say, he would have known that there is a special way of turning when you are doing a goblin spell. (It's quite complicated, so I won't go into it, but some of your fingers and two of your toes have to be crossed.)

The minute the spell was finished, Boxwood ran to the window to see if there was an extra room at the back of the house. But there was the garden, just as usual. A nasty thought occurred to Boxwood. What if the room had been added to the front of the house by mistake? He remembered that he hadn't actually told

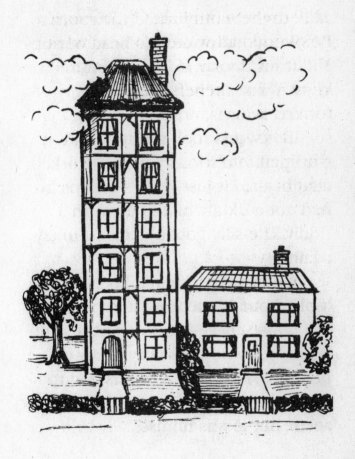

Millet where he wanted the room to be. Boxwood poked his head out of the front door and looked left and right. What a relief! Everything looked as usual.

Boxwood took a closer look at the spell. It obviously hadn't worked. Had he said it just right? Perhaps he had got a diddly mixed up with a tiddly. The silly goblin decided to try again.

But this time, when Boxwood looked out of the front and back of the house, there was no change again. Boxwood felt very disappointed. He had looked forward to surprising Dahlia. He tried again, and again, but it was no use.

When Dahlia walked back down the road that afternoon, she certainly was surprised. What silly Boxwood hadn't realised from inside the house was that the rooms had been added on top. Now Boxwood's house was the tallest in the village, and it quite obviously was not within goblin building regulations, which are not very strict but draw the line at six-storey houses.

Dahlia didn't need to think very hard to guess that Boxwood was responsible. It wasn't very long before that goblin knew exactly what his wife thought of him, too.

"You must go straight back to Millet and ask for the antidote," she said. "All spells can be undone, and this one must be dealt with before the authorities come round. After all, it's not exactly something you could walk past without noticing."

Boxwood didn't like having to go back to Millet and confess he had made a mistake, but he had no

choice. The old goblin was not at all happy when he heard what had happened.

"It's silly young goblins like you who give magic a bad name," he said. "I'm not going to trust you to undo this mess. I shall have to come down to your house myself and sort it out. Goodness me!"

So Millet walked slowly down to Boxwood's house, which turned out to be a blessing in disguise. For there, while he was putting right the six-storey problem, he met Dahlia. She was so obviously the kind of wise, sensible goblin that should be in charge of magic that Millet asked at once if he could pass his secrets on to her. He had been looking for a long time for a young goblin to train before it was too late.

That is why Dahlia is now the most respected person in town. But she keeps her magic books well away from you-know-who!

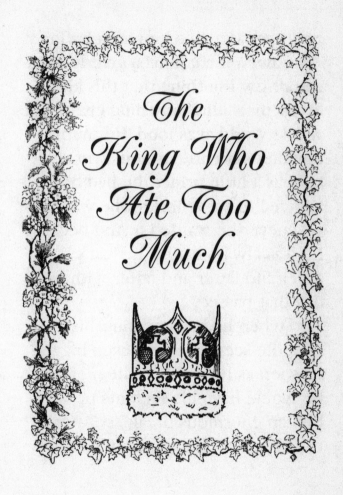

# The King Who Ate Too Much

LONG AGO, in a kingdom far, far away, there lived a greedy king. Now the thing that this king loved, more than anything else in the whole world, was food. He simply couldn't get enough of it. Ever since he was a little prince, he had been allowed to eat whatever he wanted, whenever he wanted it. And because he was always eating, he just got fatter and fatter and fatter with every day that passed.

When he became king, his appetite seemed to get even bigger! As soon as he woke in the morning, he would have his servants bring him an enormous breakfast. After eating several huge, steaming bowls of porridge, he would eat slice after slice of hot, buttered toast and jam, followed by all the boiled eggs that the royal chickens could lay.

In case he got a little hungry mid-morning, he would have a snack — usually ten or more chocolate cakes, washed down with as many cups of tea!

At lunchtime, the table would groan with the weight of all the pies, sandwiches, fruit and biscuits that the greedy king was about to gobble down.

For afternoon tea, it would be cakes, cakes and more cakes.

But the king's biggest meal was supper! The royal cooks toiled for

most of the day to prepare this feast.
When it was time for the king to eat,
one servant after another would
carry in great bowls of steaming
soup, plates of fish of every kind,
followed by huge roasts and dishes
of vegetables. Down it all went,
followed by fruit and jelly. At last, the
king would be full and he would
retire to his bed for the night.

But the king's greedy eating
habits also made him a very
thoughtless king. No-one dared tell

him that much of the wealth of the kingdom had to be spent on his huge meals. In the meantime, his loyal subjects were going hungry and becoming poor and needy.

One day, just after the king had eaten his usual big lunch, he began to feel very strange. Not only did he feel even bigger than usual, he also began to feel very light. Suddenly, without any warning, he started floating up from the table and into the air like a big balloon.

"Help! Get me down!" he cried.

The royal courtiers and servants jumped up and down and tried in vain to grab the king as he floated upwards, but in no time at all he had floated out of reach. Before anyone knew it, he had floated out of the castle window. Out across the royal grounds he went, over the river and towards the woods and mountains of his kingdom.

"Wooaa-aaah!" cried the king, as he disappeared from view.

Soon, the king began to float over a small farm. He looked down and saw the farmer's children, dressed only in rags, searching for firewood. Some thin, hungry cows stood nearby chewing on a few meagre pieces of hay. Over the next farm he floated, and a similar sad scene met his gaze. Dressed in rags, a poor farmer and his family toiled their soil hoping to grow enough to eat.

Next he floated over a small village. Everywhere he looked he saw shabby, run-down houses in need of repair and people in the streets begging for money.

Every farm and every village the king floated over told the same story of hunger and misery. The king suddenly felt very sad and very ashamed. He had been so busy enjoying himself eating that he hadn't given a thought to the plight of his subjects. While he was getting fatter and fatter, they were all getting thinner and poorer.

Now, a gust of wind was blowing the king back towards his castle. As he was passing over the castle, he suddenly felt himself falling. Down, down, he went until he landed back into the castle grounds with a great thud and a bounce.

That very day, the king sent out a royal proclamation. All his loyal subjects were to come to the castle for a huge feast, after which they would all be given a purse full of gold.

As for the king, he was never greedy again. Instead of spending all his money on food for himself, he gave enough to all the people in the land so that they would never be hungry or poor again.

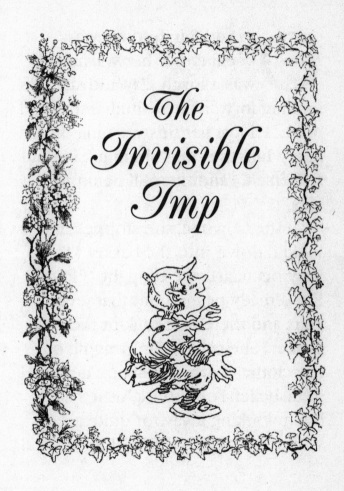

The
Invisible
Imp

ONE DAY, Sarah Jones was pegging out her washing. It was a lovely day and she was looking forward to visiting her friend Rose. "I'll just get this washing on the line while the sun's shining," she said to herself, "and then I'll be on my way."

After a while, she stopped and looked down into the basket. "That's very peculiar!" she thought. "I know I've already pegged out that green shirt and there it is back in the basket." She carried on pegging out the clothes. Now she shook her head in disbelief. For although she had been working away for quite a while, the basket of washing was still full and there was almost nothing on the line! She began to get quite cross, for she was going to be late getting to Rose's house.

Try as she might, she just could not get that washing pegged. In the end, she had to leave the basket of wet washing and run to Rose's house.

"I'm so sorry I'm late, Rose," she gasped, all out of breath from

running. Sarah told Rose all about what had happened.

"Well," said Rose, "that's a strange coincidence. I was baking some cakes for us to have for tea. Every time I put them in the oven and turned away, they were out of the oven and on the table again! In the end I had to stand guard over them — which reminds me, they were just beginning to cook nicely when you knocked on the door."

The two women went into Rose's kitchen and there were the cakes, sitting on the table again, half-cooked. "Now they're ruined!" cried Rose. "Whatever shall we do?"

At that moment, there was a

noise in the street. Rose and Sarah looked out of the window to see Elmer, the postman, surrounded by a crowd of people all shouting and waving envelopes in the air. The two women ran out into the street. "What's going on?" they cried.

"Elmer's given us all the wrong post," said Rose's neighbour, Dora. "He's normally so reliable, but this morning he seems to have gone completely crazy. Now we've got to sort out all the mail for him."

"I don't know what's happened," wailed Elmer in anguish. "I'm sure I posted all the letters through the right doors."

"Well," said Sarah, "Rose and

I have also found strange things happening to us this morning." She told the crowd their stories. Everyone forgave Elmer when they realised it wasn't his fault, but they were still truly mystified as to what — or who — could have caused all these problems.

But that wasn't the end of it. Oh no, indeed! The butcher's wife served her family mutton stew, but when she lifted the lid the family heard a bleating sound and a little lamb leaped out of the pot. The milkman delivered the milk as usual, but when people took their milk indoors, they found the bottles were full of lemonade. Old Mr Smith tried to pull his chair up to the table and found it was stuck hard to the floor. And when Mrs Smith painted her bedroom blue, she came back and found it had changed to pink with purple spots.

Can you guess what had happened? Do you know who'd been up to all these tricks? It was an imp, of course! The wicked little fellow had become bored playing pranks on the fairies and goblins in fairyland. By now, they knew all his tricks and he was finding it harder and harder to catch them out. Then he had an idea. Why not play tricks in the human world where he would be invisible? So that's exactly what he did. At first, he really only meant to play one or two tricks, but he had such fun that he couldn't resist carrying on.

Well, the invisible imp continued on with his tricks. But of course, as you know, pride comes before a fall, and one day he just went too far. Sarah Jones had been invited to a party. It was to be a fancy dress party and on the invitation it said: "Please wear red". Now Sarah fretted because she had no red clothes at all. Then she had an idea. She got out an old blue frock from the back of the cupboard. "I'll dye it red," she thought.

She mixed a big tub of red dye

and was just about to put the dress into it, when along came the invisible imp. "Here's some fun!" he thought. "I'll turn the dye blue. Then she won't know why her dress hasn't changed colour. Won't that be funny!" And he started giggling to himself at the thought of it. He danced up and down on the edge of the tub, thinking up a really evil spell to turn the dye blue. But he laughed so much to himself that he slipped and fell right into the bright red mixture. Fast as lightning out he scrambled and cast his spell.

Sure enough Sarah fished out the dress from the tub, and to her dismay saw that it was exactly the same colour as when she had put it into the dye. She was about to peer into the tub when something caught her eye. For there, sitting on the table, chuckling to himself and holding his sides with laughter, was a bright red imp. And there was a trail of tiny red footprints from the tub of dye to the table. The silly imp had no idea that he was no longer invisible and that Sarah could see him as plain as the nose on her face!

In a flash Sarah realised what had happened. She chased the imp out of the house and down the street and, I'm glad to say, he wasn't able to play his mischievous tricks ever again.

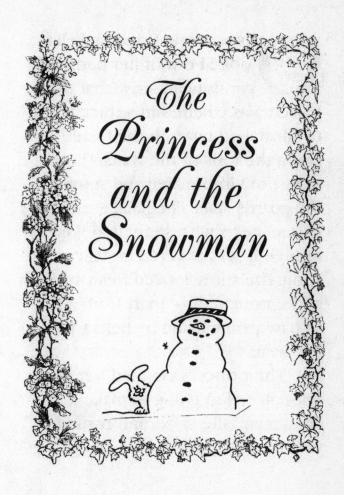

The
Princess
and the
Snowman

ONE MORNING Princess Bella looked out of her bedroom window and saw that the palace was covered in a thick layer of snow. Snow lay on the turrets and along the tops of the walls. There was snow in the well and snow on the guards' hats. The palace garden was so deep with snow it looked as though it was covered in delicious icing. The snow looked fresh, inviting and untouched — apart from a line of paw prints made by Bella's pet cat, Beau.

The princess clapped her hands with glee. "I'm going to make a snowman," she cried, and rushed off to find her warmest coat and gloves.

Soon she was busy in the garden rolling a great ball of snow for the snowman's body and another one for his head.

At last the snowman was finished, and she put an old hat on his head and a scarf around his neck.

"Now," thought Princess Bella, "he needs a face." Turning to Beau she said, "Go and find the snowman a nose."

"Meiow!" said Beau and trotted off. Bella found three lumps of coal and stuck them in a row on the snowman's head to make a mouth. Then she stuck a stone on each side of his head for ears. Beau came back with a piece of carrot in her mouth.

"Well done, Beau," said Bella. "That's perfect for a nose." And she stuck the carrot in place.

At that moment there was a call from a palace window. "Bella, Bella! Come inside at once. It's time for your lessons," called the queen. Bella

ran indoors and, do you know, she
forgot all about giving the snowman
a pair of eyes.

"I wonder when the princess
will come and give me my eyes,"
thought the snowman wistfully. "I'd
better keep my wits about me." He
listened hard with his stone ears and
sniffed with his carrot nose, but
there was no-one there.

Night came and all the lights in
the palace went out. In the middle of
the night, a storm blew up. The
windows of the palace rattled, the
trees creaked and groaned and the
wind moaned. The snowman strained
his stone ears even harder and now
he could hear a fearsome icy jangle

and a piercing, shrieking laugh. It was the Ice Queen. As she blew past the snowman, he felt the Ice Queen's cold breath on his snowy cheek and the touch of her icicle fingers on his snowy brow. The snowman shivered with fear. Now he heard the Ice Queen's icy tap, tap, tap on the palace door and her howl as she slipped through the keyhole. There was silence for a while, then suddenly the snowman heard a window being flung open and the Ice Queen's cruel laugh.

"She's leaving," thought the snowman with relief.

But what was this? Now he could hear the sound of a girl

sobbing and as the Ice Queen passed he heard Princess Bella's voice calling, "Help me!" Then there was silence again, save for the sound of the wind in the trees.

"She's carried off the princess," thought the snowman. "There's only one thing to do!" He drew his breath and with all his might he shouted through his coal lips, "Heeelp!" He thought to himself, "No-one will hear

my shouts above the noise of the wind."

But soon he felt a warm glow on his cheek. "Can I help?" said a soft, kindly voice. "I am the South Wind and I can see you're in trouble."

The snowman could hardly believe his stone ears. "Oh, yes, please help," he cried. "The Ice Queen has carried off Princess Bella and I'm afraid she may die of cold."

"I'll see what I can do," said the South Wind gently, and she started to blow a warm wind. She blew and she blew and soon the Ice Queen's icy arms began to melt. Then Bella was able to slip from her cold grasp.

"It was the snowman who saved

you," whispered the South Wind in Bella's ear as she carried her back to the palace.

Bella could hear the drip, drip, sound of snow being melted by the South Wind's warm breath. As she reached the palace gate, the sun was rising and the snow in the garden was turning to slush. "I must see my snowman before he is gone," she thought.

There he was on the lawn. His hat was starting to slide off his head and his mouth was all crooked. She rushed over to him and to her aston-ishment he spoke.

"Please give me my eyes before I melt completely," he begged.

"Yes, of course I will," Bella replied. Quickly she fixed two pieces of coal in place on his melting face.

"You are so lovely," said the snowman, looking at her with his coal eyes. "I have one last request before I'm gone. Will you marry me?"

"Why, I will!" said Bella without thinking twice — for how could she refuse the request of the one who had saved her from the Ice Queen?

Bella could not bear to think that the snowman was melting away. She glanced down so that he would not see that she was crying.

"Bella," he said. She looked up and there standing before her was a prince. For once in her life she was speechless.

"Long ago, the Ice Queen carried me away — just like she did to you. She cast a spell on me that meant I could only return to earth as falling snow. But by agreeing to marry me you have broken the spell," said the prince.

And so Bella and the prince were married, and lived happily ever after.

# The Giant Boots

TWINKLETOWN is usually a quiet place. Perhaps it's because it has such a silly name that not very much seems to happen there. The elves who live in Twinkletown generally go about their business without much fuss, and I can't remember the last time there was anything as dramatic as a fire or an

outbreak of sneezles. (In case you don't know, that's an illness only elves suffer from. It makes them giggle and sneeze at the same time, and it's quite difficult to cure.)

So, with Twinkletown being such a quiet place, you can imagine how amazed everyone was when they woke up one morning to find a pair of giant boots standing on the poppleball pitch. (I'll explain poppleball another time.)

Of course, it would be pretty astonishing to find a pair of giant boots anywhere (except on a pair of giant feet), but to find them in Twinkletown really did seem most extraordinary.

Even before breakfast (and elves, as you know, love a big breakfast), several elves had gathered around the boots.

"I've never seen anything like it," said Mugwort, who was a very old elf and had seen most things in his time, although he couldn't always remember what he had seen yesterday.

"They must have arrived in the night," gasped Umpelty, who had a genius for stating the obvious.

"Well done, Einstein," said Twig, one of the cleverer elves in Twinkle-town, which is not renowned for cleverness. "They look to me," he went on, "like giant boots."

"Well, of course they're giant boots," said Mugwort testily. "No one in his right mind would call them tiny boots."

"No," sighed Twig, "that's not what I mean. I mean they look like the kind of boots that might belong to a giant."

A very long silence greeted these words. Everyone was disturbed by the idea of a giant. Suddenly, all minds were filled with questions.

""Where's the giant?" asked Mugwort, looking anxious.

"Are giants friendly?" asked Umpelty, looking worried.

"And more to the point, wherever he is, and however friendly he is, why isn't he wearing his boots?" asked Twig.

Slowly, all three elves spun round on their heels, as if they expected to see that a bootless giant had been sneaking up behind them in his socks. But everything looked exactly as usual — except for the boots.

"We shall have to have a meeting," said Umpelty, who found it very hard to make a decision without other people telling him what to think.

"We certainly shall," said Mugwort, who welcomed any opportunity to listen to the sound of his own voice.

"I suppose so," said Twig, who knew that an elfin meeting could go on for days without coming to any very great conclusion — much like human meetings, in fact.

We have a few moments, while the elves are getting together for their meeting and arguing about which seats to sit in, so I'll tell you about poppleball. It's a very silly game indeed, which only elves would want to play (with the

possible exception of fairies, who are, if anything, sillier than elves). You have to balance a ball on the end of your nose and run backwards towards the goal, which is shaped like a laundry basket and has, for no very good reason that I've ever been able to discover, bananas painted all over it. The idea is not, as you might expect, to throw the ball into the goal, but to jump into it yourself, without dropping the ball from your nose. Unless you are cheating in the worst possible way (and most elves wouldn't dream of cheating), it is almost impossible to score. Games of poppleball invariably end with a score of 0—0, with the result that the league table is one of the most predictable items ever printed in the Elf Gazette.

Right, now the elves are settled in their seats, so we must go back to the meeting.

The first person to speak was the only elf who had ever actually met a giant. His name was Diggle, and he had once travelled a great deal.

"The giant that I met," he said, "was a really nasty piece of work. He hated anyone smaller than himself and often made them into pies. Perhaps some giants are nicer. I don't know. But what I find very strange about this whole business is that the giant I knew would never have dreamed of taking off his boots. He wore them in bed and when he took a bath (which was not very often). Why has our giant taken his boots off?"

Unfortunately, Diggle had to repeat most of his speech because almost everyone stopped listening in horror when he got to the bit about little-person-pies.

When the whole speech had finally been understood, an elf at the back of the room waved a heavy book in the air.

"I've got a dictionary here," called Parsley. "It confirms just what you say. Listen:

'Giant *n*. A very large person with unpleasant eating habits. Wears seven-league boots, which he never removes.' It sounds as though Diggle is right about the abandoned boots. Where is the giant?"

"Just a minute," put in Twig, "are those seven-league boots? They don't look much bigger than four-and-a-half-league boots to me." (And that just goes to show that Twig can sometimes talk just as much nonsense as the next elf, because I happen to know that he doesn't have the faintest idea how far a league is.)

I won't bore you with the next forty-two hours of the meeting. At

the end of them, nothing very much
had been decided and just as much
silliness was being spouted as at the
beginning. It was when Twig was
trying to raise his four-and-a-half-

league question for the nineteenth time that a small voice shouted out from the back of the hall.

"Excuse me! I say, excuse me!"

No one paid any attention at all. An argument had broken out about whether seven leagues was longer than forty-three furlongs, as if that had anything at all to do with the subject on hand — or on foot — or, actually, not on foot!

"Excuse me!" The voice came again. "Could someone come and help me with my boots?"

Again, no one paid any attention, but five minutes later, when there was a lull in the conversation, Mugwort suddenly asked, "Did someone mention boots?" And just as everyone was about to raise their eyebrows at the old man's foolishness, because, after all, they had been talking about boots for the past two days, the little voice at the back shouted again, more loudly.

"Yes!" it said. "I left some boots on your field last night and I wondered if half a dozen of you strong young elves could help me move them."

All eyes turned on the stranger, who turned out to be an ordinary looking elf with quite small feet.

To cut a long story short, the elf was a bootmaker. For the purposes of advertising his work, he had made

a pair of giant boots, which he took around with him on a truck. The night before, the truck had broken down, and rather than trying to tow it with the boots on board, the elf had decided to leave them in the field, confident that the local elves would be talking about what to do well into the middle of the week.

"The only trouble is," said the bootmaker elf, "that the truck is getting old and really can't carry more than one boot any more. I don't really need two, so I was wondering if I could leave one of them here with you."

"I'll look after it," called an old woman who had so many children she didn't know what to do, but that is another story, and you probably know it already.

So it was that the most exciting thing to happen in Twinkletown for years turned out to be about as exciting as … well … as the score at the end of a game of poppleball!

# The Travelling Tree

ONCE UPON A TIME, there was a very fine tree who lived in a forest. He was perfectly happy there, surrounded by his friends. He imagined that one day the whole forest would be cut down for timber. Then he would be carted off to a new life, and he would be able to see a little bit more of the world.

But when the time came for the forest to be felled, a very strange thing happened. All the trees around our tree were cut down, but he was left. Now, instead of standing in the middle of a forest, he stood on a huge area of open ground.

The tree could not think why

he, of all the forest, had been left,
and to tell you the truth, neither can
I, but that is what happened. At first,
the tree tried to make the best of it.
It was nice to be able to look at the
countryside, instead of seeing
nothing but other trees. But the
novelty of his situation soon wore
off. The tree was bored and lonely.
The land around stretched, flat and
barren, for miles. After being covered
with trees for so long, it was not yet
able to grow other plants. There
were not even any flowers. The tree
felt increasingly unhappy.

But what can a tree do to
improve his situation? He can't hurry
off to complain to the authorities or

find a more interesting place to live. Or can he?

The more the tree thought about it, the more convinced he became that he could move, if he only put his mind to it. Yes, I know, trees don't move. Well, they wave their branches in the wind, but they don't suddenly stroll off down the street, do they? However, our tree was determined. When he made up his mind that he wanted to move, that was it. He put all his energy into doing just that.

One fine spring morning, when anything seemed possible, the tree decided to try to move. He stood up very straight and concentrated as

hard as he could on his roots. He thought and thought and thought, and suddenly, just when he was beginning to give up hope, one of his roots gave a distinct wiggle.

The tree tried again. This time, another root gave a little twitch. This was going to be a much slower process than he had imagined. The tree realised that he was likely to have to spend quite some time doing warming-up exercises before he was ready to wander off across the open plain. But he had made a start. That was the important thing.

Over the next few weeks, the tree practised hard every day. Pretty soon, he could wiggle his roots with hardly a thought. In fact, by wiggling them all at once, he could make himself jiggle about a little on the spot. He wasn't exactly moving, but he wasn't exactly standing still, either. The tree began to feel more cheerful.

It was after several days of wiggling and jiggling that the tree thought he might be ready to try something more ambitious. He dug his front roots into the ground, lifted his back roots as high as he could, and tried to sway forward. The tree had seen people walking, and he was pretty sure he wouldn't be able to manage that. After all, people have two legs, and they sort of sway from one to the other. Trees either have lots of legs (their roots) or one leg (their trunk), depending on which way you think about it.

The tree had decided that the best way to walk would be to rock backwards and forwards, using his roots to alternately push and pull himself over the ground. His first attempt was not very successful, but it did confirm his idea that this was the way to go. He practised harder than ever over the next few weeks.

By the time the tree felt he was really ready to try to move a few paces, it was nearly autumn. The tree was desperate to begin his journey before the winter's ice made it hard to get a grip on the ground. He told himself that he would take his first steps the next day, as soon as it was light, and settled down to have a good night's sleep, so that he would be fresh in the morning.

The morning dawned bright and breezy. The tree stretched up as tall

as he could, braced his trunk, and wobbled forward.

He didn't topple over. He didn't twizzle round. No, he moved about six inches. He was on his way!

Now trees, even very athletic ones, do not move very quickly. Our tree inched his way across the plain incredibly slowly. But it was still quick enough to make a passing rabbit more surprised than he had ever been in his life. And anyone nearby would have been able to see a kind of furrow left behind the tree as he moved.

If you add together enough inches, you make a mile. And if you add together enough miles, you can go anywhere in the world you like. So it was that the tree inched its way over a small rise one day and saw a little town in the distance.

A winding road led to the town, but the tree didn't think he would be any good at walking on a road, so he set off across the fields. Even though the tree moved incredibly slowly, it still caused puzzlement to one or two local people, who were pretty sure they hadn't ever seen a tree in the fields next to the road. But what are you going to say to your friends about that? "Oh, I saw a tree where there's never been a tree before today. Isn't that strange?" I'm afraid it's you that would be thought strange.

Well, day after day, the tree crept closer and closer to the town, until he was towering over the first little cottage.

Unfortunately, the tree had never seen a cottage before. He didn't know that the people inside need to get in and out, or that it is the door that lets them do this. So the tree stood beside the cottage, right in front of the only door.

In the morning, the father of the family got ready to go to work as usual. He put on his coat and opened the door. Clunk! The door opened about two inches before it hit the tree. The man couldn't see anything through the crack in the door, so he peered through the letterbox. Then he ran up to the attic to look out of the little window there to check that he was not going completely mad. No, there was a tree standing in front of the door.

The man had a vague feeling that he'd seen just such a tree at the bottom of the garden a few weeks back. But what was it doing now blocking his door?

Always a resourceful fellow, the man rigged up some flags from the attic window, to attract the attention of passing townsfolk so that they would come to the rescue.

Sure enough, it was not long before quite a group of people had gathered in front of the cottage. As is often the case with such groups, they were much more interested in talking about what had happened and why than they were in rescuing the poor man and his family inside. "But how did it get here?" the trapped family heard someone say more than once.

"Never mind how it got here!" bellowed the man through the letterbox. "Just get us out!"

All day the discussion went on, with the family inside getting more and more aggrieved. At last the leader of the group, who also happened to be the Mayor, leaned round the tree and banged on the only part of the door he could reach.

"I say! Are you in there?" he called loudly.

I'm afraid that the reply of the cottage's owner is not in the least printable, which is not surprising really.

"We've decided what we need to do!" called the Mayor.

"Thank goodness for that!" yelled the man inside. "What?"

"What?"

"I said, what are you going to do? How long will it take?"

"Oh, we'll have to come back tomorrow," called the Mayor. "It is much too late to start now. We've decided we're going to cut the tree down."

"It's taken you all day to decide that?" yelled the man inside. And there was another unprintable bit.

The Mayor looked up. Was it his imagination, or did the tree give a kind of a shudder?

"It's a very fine tree," he called. "The kind that anyone would be glad to have in their garden."

"But not in front of their door!" The man inside was exasperated beyond belief, but he could see that there was no chance of persuading the Mayor to do anything sensible tonight.

"Oh, never mind!" he called. "But

I'll be expecting you first thing in the morning!"

Even as the townsfolk were slowly walking home, still wondering about the amazing tree, the tree itself was thinking hard. Although, in the past, he had been quite happy at the thought of being cut down, now it didn't seem such an attractive idea. He would never be able to walk across the countryside again! That was no fate for a travelling tree.

The tree waited until it was dark, then it stretched up tall and used every ounce of its energy to hurl itself away from the cottage. The tree had become very strong during its journey, and it had not moved at all during the day, so now it was feeling fresh and vigorous. You would have been astonished to see the speed with which the tree swayed across the garden and into the neighbouring field. Of course, the townsfolk would have been even more astonished, for they were still thinking that the tree had been moved by witchcraft or a freak storm.

But the tree had learned its lesson. Letting humans see what it was doing was going to be more trouble than it was worth. You never knew when they were going to have their axes with them, and although the tree could move very quickly for a tree, it could never outpace a human being.

The tree knew it would have to hide. If it could hide by day, then at night it could travel to its heart's content. Hide? I know what you are thinking. How on earth can you hide an enormous tree? You can't just throw a sheet over it and pretend it isn't there.

But the tree had learnt a lot on his travels, and now he did something very clever indeed. He got behind a thick hedge and lay down! Yes, his roots and his trunk had become so supple, he just lay down, out of sight.

So next morning, the tree-chopping party led by the Mayor was a comical sight. And the next night, the tree made good his escape.

I believe he is still on the move somewhere, and you may well have seen him. Keep an eye on the trees in your neighbourhood, and if you see a visiting one, say hello from me!

# The Wise Wizard

THERE WAS ONCE a wizard who lived deep in a forest. His life was very lonely. The only people he ever saw were travellers, journeying through the forest on their way to somewhere else.

The wizard looked forward to these meetings. He preferred to live on his own, but it was nice to see a friendly face sometimes. In winter, when the paths were clogged with snow, and travelling was hard, he often did not see a soul for three months together.

One winter's night, when the wind howled around his windows, and a nasty draught was sneaking through the floorboards, the wizard heard an urgent knock on the door.

At first, he ignored it, assuming that it was the branch of a tree or one of the other woodland sounds that come on a windy night. But the hammering came again, and this time there was no doubt about.

The wizard was very surprised. Surely the weather was much too bad for anyone to be out on a night like this?

The wizard went to the door and opened it just a crack, not because he was worried about who might be outside, but to stop the wind howling into his home and blowing his papers from this week to next. But as soon as the wizard had unlatched the door, it was pushed roughly open, and a menacing figure in furs and skins strode into the room, as the icy wind blasted past him and flurries of snow blew up around the open doorway.

By instinct, the wizard pushed the door shut again before he turned to his visitor. He did not feel afraid, but he certainly was wary and careful in what he said.

"My name is Eyebright," he said. "May I have the honour of knowing your name?"

The stranger growled. "It's none of your business," he said. "Give me something to eat."

The wizard looked carefully at the man. He could see that he had lived a rough life that had furrowed his brow and greyed his hair. He looked half dead with cold, and there was a paleness about his skin that made the wizard wonder if he was well.

The wizard also noticed that the visitor carried both a sword and a mighty axe, hanging from his belt. He had no doubt that the man would not hesitate to use them, so he went to his store cupboard and brought out bread and cheese. Then he filled a bowl with soup that had been bubbling on the stove, and put it before the hungry man.

The man ate as if he had not seen food for weeks, as indeed he had not. When he had finished, he lay back in his chair, exhausted,

although the wizard noticed that he kept one hand on his axe handle at all times.

"Have you been travelling long?" asked the wizard.

"None of your business," replied the stranger again. And he promptly fell right off the chair and collapsed on to the floor. His eyes were closed, and his breath came shallowly, as the wizard bent over him.

Eyebright could see that his first guess had been right. It was not simply cold and starvation that ailed the man. Gingerly, the wizard pulled off the sick man's great fur cloak. He gasped when he saw the deep wound in the stranger's shoulder.

Now Eyebright was not the kind of wizard who does spectacular spells or makes himself disappear. He was an everyday sort of wizard, who knew a great deal about wild plants and herbs and the movement of the stars. He had studied for years to learn the secrets of living things and the world around him. As a result, he was a very wise man.

For two months, the wizard looked after the man who had come in from the storm. During that time, the man was hardly ever conscious. In his dreams, he mumbled about battles fought and chances taken. The wizard was not at all sure that he could save the stranger's life.

Very gradually, however, the man improved. His sleep became quieter, and his head tossed less violently upon the pillow. The wound in his shoulder was healing slowly, and the spoonfuls of soup that the wizard had patiently dripped between his lips had given him new strength.

One day, watery sunshine flooded into the wizard's home. Outside his door, he picked the first small bunch of snowdrops and put it in a little pot by the stranger's bed. For the first time, the man opened his eyes and seemed to understand what he could see. As his gaze fell upon the delicate white flowers, his lips trembled into a tiny smile.

But as the man stared around, his fierce manner returned. He scowled and struggled to sit up.

"Where am I, and who are you?" he demanded, staring at the wizard's books and papers.

"I am Eyebright," explained the wizard again. "You came to me two months ago. You were cold and starving, and you had a dreadful wound in your shoulder. I have cared for you as well as I could, and I think that if you are careful, you will now recover."

The stranger was silent for a moment. "Has anyone been here?" he asked. "Who knows I am here?"

"No one," said the wizard. "The weather has been too bad for travellers to venture through the deepest parts of the forest. Now that spring is on its way, we shall see more visitors along the path."

At that, the stranger started up, wincing with pain as he staggered to his feet. He reached for his fur cloak, searching wildly for his sword and axe.

"They are here," said the wizard, holding up the weapons, "but you should not rush off so quickly. You still need rest and time for your shoulder to heal properly. If you go now, I cannot guarantee that all will be well."

With a great howl, the man leapt at the wizard, wrenching the sword and axe from his grasp and hurling him to the floor. Then he dropped to his knees and held the blade of the sword across the wizard's throat.

"If you tell anyone I have been here," he said, "I will come back one dark night and kill you. Or shall I finish you now?"

There was a long moment of silence as the sharp sword blade dug into Eyebright's throat. At first the wizard could hardly breathe, he was so frightened. Then he looked into the angry stranger's eyes and began, very softly, to speak.

"You are a brave man," he said. "From your appearance and the few words I understood you to say while you were ill, I take it that you are a soldier. That is something to be proud of. So, I must ask you, my friend, what are you afraid of?"

For a split second, fury rose in the stranger's eyes, then he released the wizard and pulled himself slowly to his feet. He let his sword drop on the floor and moved painfully over to a chair.

"Your words have pierced my heart," he said. "I am not a soldier, friend, I am a brigand. I make my living by stealing from travellers in the forest. I have killed men, and I have robbed those who could not afford to lose so much as a halfpenny. Oh, I was a soldier once, but I lost one battle after ten years of fighting for my King, and I was punished. After that, my heart became bitter. No one showed kindness to me, and I showed mercy to no one … until I met you. There is a price on my head. Sooner or later someone will kill me for my price, and that is all that I deserve."

The wizard smiled at the stranger. "And do you plan to continue in your old life, when you leave here?" he asked, pouring a drink for the visitor.

"No," said the man, "for my heart is no longer in it. You have reminded me of the way I used to live, trying to do what is right, helping people where I could. I cannot go back to stealing and killing now. But it is too late for me. The next traveller to pass will recognise me for sure, and it will all be over. The King's men will cut me down."

"You are too weak to travel at the moment," said the wizard, "but I feel sure that you could make a new life for yourself in another country. In the meantime, I think I know how we can make sure that no passer-by recognises you."

And that is why, when travellers stopped for a drink and crust of bread at the wizard's door that spring, they found the wizard seemed taller and stronger in his robes, though he was as kindly and welcoming as ever.

In midsummer, the wizard and the brigand parted company. No one would have recognised the clean-shaven man in forest green who strode along the path towards a new life.

The wizard watched him go with a smile. Then he went back to his quiet and sometimes lonely ways. To this day, he is wise enough to see some goodness in everyone he meets, and somehow, that means that there is simply more goodness to go around.

Goodnight,
Little
Elf

Once upon a time, there was a little elf who lived in a tree. It was a beautiful big house, with a smart door and four little windows at the front. The elf loved her home, but it was rather old. One day storm clouds gathered and a great wind swept through the forest. With a creaking and a crashing, the tree-trunk house tumbled to the ground. Luckily its branches cushioned the fall, and it fell with its windows pointing to the sky, so the little elf was not hurt and managed to climb out of her own front door. But her beloved home was lost for ever.

Now elves live in all kinds of

places. You will find them in toadstools and among the roots of
hedgerows. They may borrow an
abandoned bird's nest or make a
cosy house in a deserted rabbit's
burrow. In fact, they can live almost
anywhere. The only place that elves
really don't like to live is somewhere
that has humans nearby. Elves are
always a little bit afraid that humans
will try to catch them and keep
them captive. Perhaps they are right.

The little elf in this story, whose
name was Periwinkle, set to work
straight away to find a new place to
live. She was very sad to leave her
old home, but she really didn't have
any choice. She was always a happy,

practical little elf, so she made the best of the situation and began her search.

Unfortunately, it wasn't very easy. The storm had happened just as winter was passing into spring, and in springtime, as you know, little creatures are all finding or building homes to have their babies in.

It seemed to poor Periwinkle that every burrow she looked in had a mother rabbit already in residence. And every nest that she thought was abandoned had a bright-eyed little bird making essential repairs before the important egg-laying season.

What about toadstools? I hear you asking. Well, it was a strange thing, but there just didn't seem to *be* many that year. It's like that with living things. Some years there seem to be, say, ladybirds everywhere, and sometimes you can hardly find any.

The nights were still cold in early spring, so Periwinkle really needed somewhere cosy to spend the night. Luckily, she had lots of woodland friends who let her snuggle down on their floors for a night or two, but Periwinkle knew that they too would soon have houses full of little ones, and there would be no room for her. She really did need to find a home of her own.

Then, one afternoon, when Periwinkle was searching on the

very edge of the wood, she came to a wire fence. It was the kind that has great big holes in it, so it was easy for the little elf to climb through. The other side of the fence looked very wild and overgrown, so she didn't think for a moment that it might be part of a human garden.

Periwinkle made her way through the long grass. There were one or two old apple trees, but they looked as though no one was looking after them. There were some brambles and thistles, but they both looked rather prickly for an elf's home.

Suddenly, Periwinkle saw a little house in a tree! It wasn't as nice as

her old home at all, but it made
Periwinkle's eyes light up all the
same. It would be lovely to live in a
tree again!

The trunk was surprisingly easy
to climb, so the little elf quickly
clambered up it and peeped into the
little house.

It looked as though it hadn't
been lived in for a very long time.
There was no furniture and there

were no curtains at the single
window. In fact, the treehouse was
completely empty.

Periwinkle could hardly contain her excitement. It wasn't ideal for an elf, being rather high and draughty, but it was in a tree and it was empty. She would move in straight away!

Over the next few weeks, Periwinkle made the treehouse as comfortable as she could. It wasn't possible to do much about the open door and window, although she did have a word with one or two friendly spiders and asked them to spin their webs across the openings to shut out the whistling wind just a little.

But Periwinkle soon made herself some furniture from acorns and twigs. Before a week had passed, she had a chair, a table and a little bed. The treehouse was beginning to feel like home!

As Periwinkle worked on her new house, spring passed. The weather became warmer and the nights grew lighter. Soon it didn't matter that the wind could blow through the window and door. It was pleasant to have a cool breeze on her face when the sun was at its hottest.

Periwinkle was now so happy in her new home that she never even thought about who had built it. So one summer's evening, she was very, very surprised to hear someone big and heavy climbing up the tree.

Bare as the treehouse was, there
was nowhere for the little elf to hide.
She stared in horror as the face of a
big human boy appeared at the door.
In seconds, his big human body
followed. He seemed to fill the whole
treehouse as he came clumping
across the floor. And then he noticed
Periwinkle.

"Hello!" he said.

Periwinkle wanted to run away,
but the boy was between her and
the door. She wanted to hide, but
there was nowhere to go. Most of all,
she wanted to disappear into thin
air, but although elves are very clever
at a great many things, they can't do
magic like that.

So Periwinkle really didn't have much choice but to talk to the human. He seemed huge, but she realised that he was probably not very old at all, and he did *look* friendly.

"Hello," said Periwinkle in her turn. "How do you do?"

"I'm very well, thank you," said the boy politely. "Are you a fairy?"

"Goodness me, no!" said Periwinkle. "Fairies are quite different. I'm an elf. We don't have wings, you see, and we're much more sensible than fairies."

"Hmm, I always thought fairies were rather silly," said the boy. "It's interesting that you agree with me."

He looked around the tidy treehouse and saw Periwinkle's little chair, table and bed. He even noticed the cobwebs across the window. (I'm afraid he had broken the ones across the door when he came in.) For a human, he really was quite observant, thought Periwinkle.

"Have you been here long?" asked the boy.

"Since early spring," said the little elf. She was feeling much more comfortable now. He didn't look like the kind of boy who was going to put her in a jar and show her to all his friends. The next thing she knew, she was telling him all about her beloved treehouse and the great storm that had destroyed it.

"I remember that night," said the boy. "Our gates were blown right off their hinges."

There was a small silence. Then the boy said, "I'm Jake, by the way. Who are you?"

"Periwinkle," said the little elf. "I'm very pleased to meet you, although I've never spoken to a human before."

"If it comes to that," laughed the boy, "I've never spoken to an elf! This has been quite a day."

Well, the little elf and the boy talked for a long , long time, until they heard his mummy's voice calling from the other end of the garden. "Jake! Jake! Where are you?"

At once, Periwinkle looked frightened out of her wits. "What's the matter?" asked Jake. "It's only my mother. She's quite nice really."

Then Periwinkle explained about how elves are afraid of humans, and the boy looked as if he understood.

"There are things that I'm afraid of too," he said. "And you don't have to worry about me telling anyone about you. I think my friends would laugh, you know. I don't think boys are meant to see elves, any more than elves are meant to talk to boys. You can be a secret."

"And you can be a secret, too," said the little elf. "My elf friends wouldn't like it if they knew I talked to you either."

"Well, I must go now," said Jake. "But I'll come and see you again tomorrow, if that's all right."

"That will be *lovely*," said Periwinkle. "Goodnight, boy!"

"Goodnight, little elf!" laughed Jake. "Goodnight!"

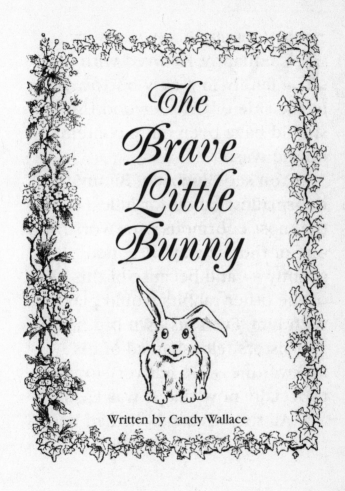

# The Brave Little Bunny

Written by Candy Wallace

BLUEBERRY BUNNY was very unhappy. He lived with his family, in a cosy burrow, deep in the side of Cricklewood Hill. He should have been quite content, but he wasn't.

You see Blueberry Bunny was the smallest rabbit for miles, with the most enormous ears. Worse still one of them always drooped slightly — and because of this none of the other rabbits would play with him. Even his own brothers and sisters felt ashamed of his awkwardness. He felt very lonely, especially now that it was Easter.

All the other rabbits had been excited for days at the thought of

the Easter Egg Hunt. The chocolate eggs that were to be hidden on Easter Sunday had been given to Mrs. Clutterbuck hen at Cricklewood Farm for safe keeping. But now there was uproar at the farm — not only had the special eggs been stolen, but also Mrs. Clutterbuck's four new chicks. Everyone agreed that it had to be the work of naughty Rufus Fox. They were all very upset.

"Can't you do something about it?" one of the young rabbits asked Ragwort. Ragwort was the strongest, biggest rabbit in the neighbourhood. He was also the most unpleasant.

"You have to be joking!" said Ragwort shaking his head. "No one with any sense would pay *him* a visit."

"But someone has to do something," said a small voice. All heads turned and stared at the speaker,

sitting a short distance away. It was Blueberry. Ragwort burst out laughing.

"Just listen to that!" he jeered. "And from someone who's even frightened of his own shadow!" Blueberry winced. It was true — lots of things scared him.

"Blueberry Bunny, Blueberry Bunny! Whatever he does, he always looks funny." Ragwort chanted loudly, and thumped his paw heavily on the ground.

Blueberry stood up and slunk off in the direction of Cricklewood Forest — the noise of laughter ringing in his ears. Two big tears plopped onto his whiskers. Blindly he stumbled into the undergrowth, and flopped down in between the tangled roots of a huge tree.

"It's not fair!" he whimpered, wiping his wet fur.

"I quite agree!" A hooting voice, just above Blueberry's head made him jump. Blueberry looked up and there, on a branch, sat the most miserable owl he had ever seen.

"Shouldn't you be in bed at this time of day?" asked Blueberry, surprised to see a night owl awake.

"That's just it," moaned the owl. "The fact of the matter is — I can't sleep." He flew down on to the ground near Blueberry and held out a wing. "Allow me to introduce myself," he said. "I am Oscar Owl."

"And I am Blueberry Bunny," said Blueberry, shaking the owl's wing.

"How do you do Blueberry," said Oscar. "And what appears to be the problem?"

"*I'm* the problem," said Blueberry mournfully, "just look at me!" Oscar craned his neck forward and stared so hard that Blueberry could feel himself turning red.

"Well..." Oscar began, "... apart from the ears and your small size... apart from that, I can't see what's wrong."

"Isn't that enough?" Blueberry squealed.

"My dear chap!" said Oscar "at least you don't have my awful problem!"

"What's that?" asked Blueberry.

"The fact of the matter is," Oscar whispered, "that I'm not very good at giving advice and helping people."

"But I thought *all* owls could help people. They do in all my story-books," said a puzzled Blueberry.

"That's just it," said Oscar miserably. "Everyone *expects* me to be wise — like storybook owls — and I'm a miserable failure. Why, only this morning, Cock-o-Dandy came to see me about his missing chicks, and I... I simply did not know what to say."

"Perhaps we could think of something together," said Blueberry, who did not like to see Oscar looking so sad. For a long while the pair sat quietly, both thinking hard.

Suddenly, Oscar broke the silence:

"I've got it! I could try to find Rufus Fox's hideout and see if the chicks are there." Blueberry nodded his head. "Then if they *are*, at least we can tell Cock-o-Dandy where to find them." Oscar looked really pleased with himself, but Blueberry shook his head.

"That's not any good. None of the farm birds, not even the great Cock-o-Dandy, would go far into Cricklewood Forest — let alone near that wicked fox. Why even Ragwort is scared of him!"

"I told you I wasn't wise!" said Oscar looking glum again.

"But you are. It's a very good idea of yours to find the hideout. If we *both* went, you could distract Rufus Fox, while I rescue the chicks," said Blueberry, forgetting his usual cowardliness.

"But *how* will you rescue them?"

"I don't know yet, but we'll think of something," said Blueberry.

Just then Blueberry noticed that the sun was going down.

"I'd better be going home now," he said, suddenly feeling scared. "I'll come back early tomorrow."

"Good idea!" said Oscar.

The next morning Blueberry's mother was surprised to see him up and dressed so early. Just as the sun was rising, he set off for Cricklewood Forest.

Oscar was sitting on the same branch as the night before, waiting for him. He yawned widely.

"I've spent most of the night reading *Sammy Squirrel's Riddle Book*," he said sleepily. It struck Blueberry as a very strange way to spend the night, but he didn't want to say so.

"And that's not all," said Oscar, hardly able to contain his excitement. "I've found Rufus Fox's hideout, and what's more Mrs. Clutterbuck's chicks *are* there."

"Did you see them then?" asked Blueberry.

"No, but Rufus was outside very late last night, gathering herbs, and I heard him muttering to himself about how parsley and sage would go very nicely with baby chicken!" Blueberry shuddered. "I think we'd better get going quickly," he said. "Before it's too late!"

Deeper and deeper the pair travelled through the woods. Blueberry didn't like the gloom, or the silence, very much. On and on they went until Blueberry could hardly see where he was going. He kept on tripping over tangled tree roots and crashing into scratchy bushes. It was only the thought of the poor baby chicks that made him determined to carry on.

Eventually the pair halted. To Blueberry's surprise, ahead he could see nothing but dark green pools — murky water surrounded by reeds and plants. Now, the one thing Blueberry was really scared of was water. So you can imagine how he felt when Oscar pointed out Rufus Fox's hideout, sitting on a tiny island surrounded by a big pool. Blueberry groaned.

"Shush!" whispered Oscar, pointing his wing toward the island. There, outside a rickety shack, was the fox lighting a fire beneath an enormous cooking pot.

"But I don't like water," whispered Blueberry.

"Pooh!" said Oscar rather unkindly. "There's nothing to be afraid of!"

"Not for you maybe, you can fly over it."

"Well, you can walk over it," said Oscar. "There are some stepping stones on the other side."

The pair skirted around the island until they were facing the

back of Rufus' shack. And there, sure enough, were the stepping stones, just visible through the reeds.

"But even so..." began Blueberry, who didn't like the look of the slippery stones. "How can I get through the front door of the shack without Rufus seeing me?"

"I've thought of that," said Oscar proudly. "The fact of the matter is, that if you'd been just one teansy-weansy bit bigger then we would have been stuck, but being as small as you are, you can get through that tiny hole at the bottom." Oscar pointed to the back of the shack. The hole was so small Blueberry hadn't noticed it.

"But what if Rufus goes inside when I'm in there?" The thought made Blueberry quiver and quake.

"Don't worry about that. That is where the riddles come in," said Oscar mysteriously. "And when you have rescued the chicks, hide them in this hollow tree and hoot like an owl." He pointed his beak toward a large tree behind them.

Before Blueberry had time to protest any further, or to tell Oscar that he couldn't hoot, his friend had flapped his wings and disappeared.

Rufus Fox was bending over the cooking pot, when Oscar landed on a branch above his head.

"Good morning, Mr. Rufus!" hooted Oscar loudly, making Rufus jump. "And what a beautiful day it is."

"It's a more beautiful day than you think," said Rufus slyly, casting a wicked glance back at his shack,

and wiping his hands on his dungarees.

"Yes siree! A very tasty day!" he grinned, showing a row of needle sharp teeth. "But I'm surprised to see you up Mr. Owl — don't your kind usually sleep when the sun's up?"

"The fact of the matter is Mr. Rufus, that I could not sleep. You see, I came across a number of riddles and, for the life of me, I can't work them out. So I thought to myself, 'Who do I know who is clever. Oh yes! I'll go and see Mr. Rufus — he's clever', I thought."

"Well now, you've sure come to the right place," said Rufus, flattered at being thought clever. "I like a good riddle and it will pass the time away until my water is ready." He sat down on a fallen log and grinned his evil grin.

"What shines but is never polished?" asked Oscar.

"That's easy! The sun, of course," Rufus answered quickly.

Better give him a hard one, thought Oscar.

"What is the biggest ant in the world'?"

Rufus had to think hard, but finally he got it.

"A giant."

Oscar looked deliberately blank.

"A GI-ANT — get it?"

Meanwhile, Blueberry was wobbling on the second stepping stone. The next stone seemed a long way off. He dared not think about how deep, or how cold, the water was. Gritting his teeth he took a deep breath and...FLUMPETYJUMP, he landed safely. Just one more to go and he would be on the island. He wobbled a bit more then, holding his breath he leaped forward again. FLUMPETYJUMP, FLUMPETYJUMP! He had made it!

Keeping as low to the ground as possible, he crept toward the back of the shack. Very quietly he squashed himself through the tiny hole. For the first time in his life, he was glad he was so small and that his ears were bendy.

Inside, in the gloom, Blueberry could see a sack by a pile of potatoes — something inside it was wriggling! Quickly he undid the piece of string at the top and lifted out the startled chicks, one by one. They blinked and were about to cheep cheerily when Blueberry held up his paw. "Shush!" He pointed to the tiny ho!e. As fast as he could, he pushed each one through. Then he placed four potatoes in the sack, did up the string and looked around for the stolen eggs. He found them in a bag in the corner, which he had to push hard through the tiny hole. Finally, he squeezed himself through and joined the chicks.

"I'm going to carry you over to that tree," he whispered. "No one must utter even the smallest cheep, or we will all get eaten by the fox!" They all closed their beaks tightly, in fright!

Blueberry bravely carried each chick over, one by one, taking the eggs with him on the first crossing. Once they were in the tree, he opened his mouth and made a very strange sound — a little like a hoot but more like a croak! Nevertheless, Oscar heard it and heaved a great sigh of relief — he was running out of riddles.

"Well, I'll be off now Mr. Rufus," he said as casually as possible, "and thank you for helping me." He couldn't resist adding, "In fact, you have been more help than you realize!"

Rufus headed into his shack and dragged the sack outside. It seemed heavier, but perhaps it was just his memory playing tricks. Meanwhile Oscar had flown straight to the hollow tree.

"Quick! Two of you climb onto my back. I'll be back for you others as soon as I can."

As he soared high above the

tree tops he looked down and
hooted:

"Stay hidden!"

Fortunately Rufus Fox didn't
hear him, for just at that moment
he discovered what was really in
his sack and let out a huge, angry
roar. Every animal in the forest
heard it.

"SOMEONE'S STOLEN MY
LUNCH! WAIT 'TIL I GET MY
TEETH INTO THEM!" Then it
dawned on him. "THAT OWL! THAT
STUPID, BLITHERING OWL. HE
KEPT ME BUSY WHILE...WHILE..."
He was so angry that he could not
spit the words out. Roaring loudly,
he began leaping around the fire,

stamping his feet with rage. He was so furious that he didn't look where he was going and the next minute he hopped RIGHT INTO THE FIRE!

"Yao. . .ow!" he screeched in pain as he hopped and limped on his sizzling feet over to the water to cool them down.

Blueberry and the chicks heard all the noise and huddled closer together inside the tree waiting for Oscar. Suddenly, they heard a whirr of wings and he was back. The last two chicks scrambled onto his back.

"Hold tight with your claws and beaks!" he warned them as he took off into the sky again.

Blueberry was now alone, but he set off through the trees quite happily. The woods were still dark, but he was no longer afraid. He knew that he wasn't the coward he had once thought he was. After all, hadn't he managed to overcome his fear of water and make the fierce fox look very foolish?

What a sound met Blueberry's ears as he came out of the trees onto Cricklewood Hill. Down below him, all the animals and birds had gathered to welcome him and were cheering at the tops of their voices.

"HOORAY FOR BLUEBERRY! BRAVO BLUEBERRY!"

Cock-o-Dandy had spread the word. Blueberry turned bright red as a crowd of rabbits rushed forward and lifted him onto their shoulders. Mrs. Clutterbuck came toward him beaming and clucking loudly.

"I can never thank you enough! I can never thank you enough!" she huffed and puffed over and over again.

"It was Oscar's plan," said Blueberry. "I couldn't have done it without his wise ideas."

"But my dear friend, the fact of the matter is, that if you hadn't been so small and so very, *very* brave, my plan would never have worked."

"Three cheers for the two heroes," Cock-o-Dandy crowed loudly, and everyone cheered again. Everyone, that is, except for Ragwort. He slunk away, annoyed that he was no longer the centre of attention.

"They'll forget all about him

tomorrow," he consoled himself. But they didn't. The next morning everyone wanted to play with Blueberry and asked him to be the leader of the Easter Egg Hunt. And he was never lonely — or cowardly — again.

# The Imprisoned Princess

LONG AGO there lived a Princess who was good, and kind, and beautiful. She was loved by everyone who knew her.

The Princess was an only child. She would inherit the kingdom after her father the King. Although the whole country was very happy at the thought of so gracious a Queen ruling them in due course, one person schemed and plotted every day to make sure that the day of the Princess's coronation never arrived.

It was the King's sister, Lady Eldred. She also had one child, a pale boy called Ghent. She was determined that he, not the

Princess, would succeed to the royal throne.

Now Lady Eldred had tried for years to show the Princess in a bad light, but she only ever succeeded in making herself look silly. When she was at her wits' end, she decided to call on greater powers than her own. She went to visit the Witch of the Wood, a woman so evil and cold that leaves shrivelled on the trees as she passed. Even Lady Eldred felt a shiver of fear as she approached the witch's lair, but she knew that she had too much to lose to turn back.

At the sound of footsteps on the woodland path, the Witch of the Wood emerged. She cackled horribly and nodded her hideous head at her visitor.

"I know why you have come, my lady," she hissed, "and I am pleased to see you." Little Miss Princess Perfect has long been gnawing at my heart. Such goodness should not be allowed to exist. I will be only too happy to help to extinguish it."

"She will need to be done away with altogether," said Lady Eldred. "She has too high a place in people's

hearts now to be toppled from her throne. What did you have in mind? I will help you all I can."

"No, no, my dear," laughed the witch, "you will *pay* me all you can. I will handle the magic by myself. Although her spirit is too strong for me to take her life, the Princess can still be captured. I will imprison her inside a tree at the heart of the wood. She will stay there for ever. Your boy can become King, and the people will forget all about the sweet-as-sugar Princess."

"That is just what I wish," said Lady Eldred. "I will bring the Princess into the wood tomorrow. You can do your worst then."

The next day was bright and sunny. It was not difficult for Lady Eldred to persuade her niece to walk with her through the lovely shade of the nearby wood. They left the castle together before midday.

When they had wandered for several hours beneath the green boughs, the Princess suggested that they should return home. But they had not yet reached the witch's lair, so Lady Eldred begged her niece to follow just one more woodland path.

"Ahaaah!" cried the Witch of the Wood, leaping across their path. "One of you two ladies must pay with her life for walking in my woodland. Which one is it to be?"

The Princess at once rushed forward to save her aunt. Her kind heart had only one wish — to protect those she loved.

"So," hissed the witch, "you have made your choice."

Her gnarled old fingers flew into the air like bats and hovered over the Princess's head. As the spell was said, the Princess's body changed.

Rough bark grew around it, while the tendrils of her hair became branches and leaves. Soon not even her loving father would have recognised her. Only her spirit, too strong for the witch's power, remained free, throwing a golden glow around the tall and stately tree she had become.

The Lady Eldred returned to the castle in tears.

"I begged her not to stray from the path," she said, "but she would not listen. One moment I could see her. The next she was gone. I searched and searched, but I could not find the Princess."

At once the King sent out all his men to comb the forest for the missing girl. But although they searched every pathway and clearing, and passed several times under the branches of a particularly beautiful tree at the very heart of the wood, they returned to the castle without their master's daughter.

For weeks, the King hoped that his child would be returned to him, happy and well, but as time passed, he had to agree with his people that she had probably been dragged away by a wild animal. He knew that he would probably never see her again.

Meanwhile, something strange was happening in the wood. The Princess's spirit, hovering over her imprisoned body, warmed the trees around it. The whole woodland became so filled with sunshine and warmth that the witch's presence was much easier to spot. Around her lair, the trees shrivelled and died. Wherever she walked through the forest, the moss blackened beneath her feet, and trees shed their leaves as though winter was on its way.

Working in the wood, there was a young woodcutter. He noticed the changes among the trees and realised at once that something evil

was lurking there. But he saw other trees flourish and turn their faces to the light, so he knew that something very valuable had come into the woodland as well.

Then, one day, the woodcutter noticed a tree he had never seen before. It was so beautiful that it took his breath away, and it made him feel at once happy and sad. He longed to stay beside it for ever, and laughed at himself for feeling so strongly about a tree that his work would one day cause him to cut down.

Nevertheless, the woodcutter spent as much time near the tree as he possibly could. One day, as he sat beneath its branches, eating his lunchtime bread and cheese, a little breeze danced through the leaves. It was as though the tree was speaking to him. "*Free me. Free me,*" it breathed. "*Free me. Free me.*"

The woodcutter sprang to his feet. "How?" he cried. "I will do anything, anything at all."

The tree spoke no more, but it came into the woodcutter's mind what he must do. He must cut down the beautiful tree!

For a long time, the young man resisted the idea. He could not bear to destroy something so lovely, but the voice in his head insisted. He knew that he would have no peace until he had carried out the dreadful act.

With tears in his eyes, the woodcutter swung his axe. It sank with a horrible thud into the body of the tree. Tears were streaming down the young man's face as he worked on. Over and over, the silvery blade of his axe swung through the air. At last, with a heartrending shriek, the tree fell to the ground — and a beautiful girl seemed to rise from its ruins. It was the Princess, freed from the witch's spell.

"So much of the witch's magic was holding me in the tree," she explained. "I knew that if the tree was killed, she too would die."

The woodcutter looked around him. The moss that had been black was fresh and green again. The trees that had shrivelled were putting out new shoots and reaching towards the sky.

"I think she is dead," he said, "but how did you survive?"

"I was not thinking of myself," said the Princess gently, "perhaps that is why the witch's death freed me as well. Whatever the reason, I have a very great deal to thank you for."

"Let me take you safely to your home," said the woodcutter, taking the Princess's hand. "There is no need to thank me."

But somewhere along the

woodland path, the Princess realised that she wished never to part from the handsome young man, and he had fallen just as much in love with her.

The King was so overjoyed to see his lost daughter again that he hardly blinked when she told him she was about to marry a woodcutter.

"Splendid!" he said. "It's time there was some new blood in our family tree. Oh, I say, did you hear that? A woodcutter in a family tree! That's rather funny."

Chuckling at his own joke, the King led the happy couple to the Great Hall, where Lady Eldred sat sewing by the fire, dreaming of the crown that would one day sit upon the head of her son.

At the sight of the Princess, Lady Eldred rose to her feet. The colour flooded from her face, and she would have fallen, if the King had not put out a hand to catch her.

"It is a shock, isn't it?" he said. "But such a happy one. How glad you must be to see your lost niece again."

But for the first time in her life, Lady Eldred showed her true colours. All the hatred she had felt for the Princess came tumbling out of her mouth. Even her son was pale with disgust.

So it was that Lady Eldred watch-ed the festivities for the marriage of her niece from the tower in which she had been imprisoned. She felt that the wheel had turned full circle, for as the daughter of a King, she too was an imprisoned Princess.

MISS LAVINIA BLENKINSOP was a very proper and particular lady. She ate her fruit with a knife and fork and always wore just the right amount of discreet jewellery. Her only regret was that the rest of her family was not so genteel. She tried not to let her friends meet them.

Then, one day, Miss Lavinia Blenkinsop had news that her Uncle Boris had died. She remembered how Uncle Boris had bounced her on his knee when she was a child. It was a shame, even though she hadn't seen the old rogue for years. Uncle Boris had been a sea captain in his youth and had sent his niece postcards from every part of the world. Rather unexpectedly, prim and proper Lavinia had had a soft spot for Uncle Boris.

A few days later, a van pulled up outside Lavinia Blenkinsop's immaculate gateway.

"Sign here, please," said the delivery man, carrying a large parcel with a big sign on it saying "This way up."

Miss Blenkinsop was very surprised, but she carried the parcel into the house and put it on the table. She saw that there was an envelope attached to it.

"Dear Miss Blenkinsop," said the letter inside, "under the terms of your uncle's last will and testament, this bird now belongs to you. It was your uncle's dearest possession, and he particularly requested that you should take good care of it."

Miss Blenkinsop smiled. A stuffed bird! How typical of Uncle Boris. Well, she needn't put it anywhere that anyone could *see* it. She undid the parcel, wondering if it would be a penguin from the North Pole or a flamingo from North Africa.

It wasn't. It was a parrot from South America — and it was alive!

Miss Lavinia Blenkinsop stared at the parrot, and the parrot stared at her.

"I'm a parrot!" he said, quite distinctly, in a loud voice.

Well, Miss Blenkinsop could see that. She had no idea how to look after a parrot, but she supposed that for Uncle Boris's sake she would have to learn. And after all, he would be a talking point. None of her prim and proper friends had parrots.

That afternoon, Miss Lavinia Blenkinsop had invited a select little party to tea. She placed the parrot in his cage prominently in the corner of the room and sat back to await reactions. She was not disappointed.

"My dear, how quaint!" said one lady in a large hat.

"What a novel idea! Isn't he a lot of trouble?" asked another.

"Not at all," said Miss Lavinia Blenkinsop. "He's as good as gold."

"Knickers!" said the parrot.

Yes, that's right. That's exactly what the parrot said, and just in case his shocked audience didn't understand him the first time, he said it again, even louder.

Miss Lavinia Blenkinsop turned pink, but she thought quickly.

"It's a Brasilian word," she said, "meaning 'Pleased to meet you.'"

The parrot made a rude noise.

"How clever he is," said his new owner. "That's a very polite term among the people of the Amazon."

Over the next few weeks, Miss B. tried to teach the parrot more polite terms, but you would be amazed how many Brasilian and Amazonian words he knew. And you would be amazed, too, if you could see how he made his owner laugh in private. It seems she had more in common with her Uncle Boris than she had realised.

So the parrot turned out not to be a problem after all. He has learnt lots of new words now — and so has Miss Lavinia Blenkinsop!

# Granny Gumdrop

**B**ELINDA climbed on to a chair and looked out of the window, as she did every day just after lunch. She held on tightly so that she didn't fall.

"Can you see her?" asked Ben.

"Yes, here she comes!" said Belinda with a giggle.

"Is she wearing her hat?"

"Yes!"

"Is she wearing her old coat?"

"Yes!"

"Has she got her boots on?"

"Yes!"

"And…?" Ben was giggling too.

"And she's got her umbrella. And it's open, it really is!"

"Silly Granny," said Ben.

The children took it in turns each day to look out of the window at the old lady. She wasn't really their granny, but they thought she looked so funny that they had nicknamed her Granny Gumdrop. They weren't usually unkind children. It was just funny the way she always dressed as if it was pouring with rain, even in the middle of the summer. Belinda and Ben had no idea that Granny Gumdrop could see them watching her as she went past.

But one day, when they were in the supermarket with their mum, the children were surprised to see a familiar figure coming round a stack of baked beans.

"It's Granny Gumdrop!" hissed Belinda, so loudly that the old lady couldn't fail to hear her.

"Why," said Granny Gumdrop, "if it isn't Hurly and Burly."

"Those aren't our names," said Ben, rather offended.

"No," said the old lady, "but Granny Gumdrop isn't *my* name. Why do you call me that, Hurly?"

Ben was younger than his sister and often alarmingly truthful.

"Because you wear a funny hat and funny clothes," he said.

"And do you want to know why I do that?" asked Granny.

"Yes," said Belinda and Ben.

"Well, why are you wearing a clown suit, Hurly? And why have you got that red hat on, Burly?" asked Granny Gumdrop.

"Because we like them," said

Belinda stoutly. "Why shouldn't we wear what we like?"

"That's exactly what *I* say," said Granny Gumdrop. "I *like* my hat, and my coat, and my boots. And I specially like my old umbrella. Why shouldn't I wear what I like?"

The children looked thoughtful, and Mummy smiled and invited their new friend to tea.

"That would be a pleasure too," said Granny Gumdrop.